BAWSHOU RESCUES THE SUN

A HAN FOLKTALE

CHUN-CHAN YEH & ALLAN BAILLIE

WITH ILLUSTRATIONS BY

MICHELLE POWELL

SCHOLASTIC
HARDCOVER

SCHOLASTIC INC.

NEW YORK

Thousands of years ago the land
was rich and peaceful . . .

Liu Chun and his wife Hui Niang worked a paddy by the shining West Lake in Eastern China.

Under the warm sun Liu Chun watched his rice plants grow heavy with grain, and Hui Niang waited for the birth of their first child.

They were content.

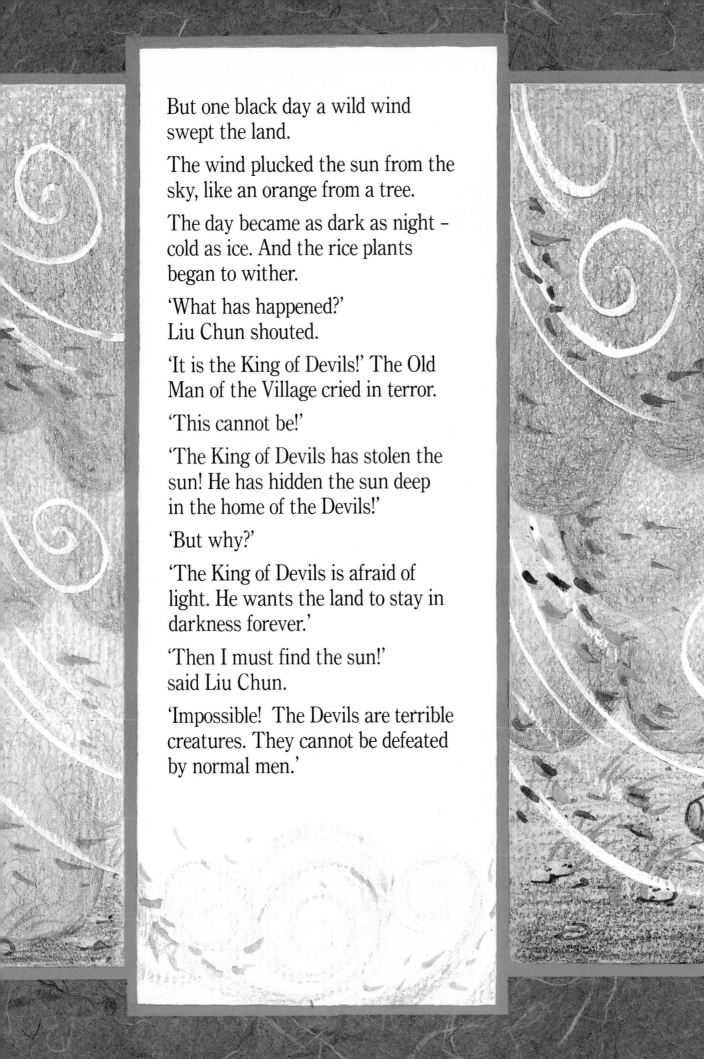

But one black day a wild wind swept the land.

The wind plucked the sun from the sky, like an orange from a tree.

The day became as dark as night – cold as ice. And the rice plants began to wither.

'What has happened?'
Liu Chun shouted.

'It is the King of Devils!' The Old Man of the Village cried in terror.

'This cannot be!'

'The King of Devils has stolen the sun! He has hidden the sun deep in the home of the Devils!'

'But why?'

'The King of Devils is afraid of light. He wants the land to stay in darkness forever.'

'Then I must find the sun!'
said Liu Chun.

'Impossible! The Devils are terrible creatures. They cannot be defeated by normal men.'

But Liu Chun was determined to try.

Hui Niang made special walking shoes for him
from her flowing hair.

And as Liu Chun said farewell to her,
a golden phoenix landed lightly on his shoulder.

'This is a good omen,' he said, and smiled.
'We will find the sun, this bird and I.
And if I fail I will show the way.'

So Liu Chun began his quest – a rice farmer
with a golden bird on his shoulder.

Hui Niang waited for months in darkness.

She was anxious and alone, until her house shook
with the laughter of a baby son.

She was delighted with the baby and called him
Bawshou. She wished Liu Chun would hurry back
so she could present him with his new son.

But one day the golden phoenix returned alone.
And a new star shone in the black sky.

Hui Niang looked at the new star, and wept.

At that moment a strange breeze touched Bawshou.
And the baby stood and spoke.

A second breeze whispered, and Bawshou
strode from the house.

A third breeze sighed. Bawshou grew
into a giant of a man.

The golden phoenix settled on his shoulder.

'Do not worry, Mother,' Bawshou boomed.
'We will find the sun. And we will release it.'

Bawshou left Hui Niang alone outside her dark house and followed the new star across the great land.

He walked through thick forests, swamps, over jagged mountains, along dusty paths, until his shoes had worn from his feet and his clothes hung in rags from his back.

But as he shuffled along a lonely road the people of a small mountain village saw him shivering, and stopped him. They made him a cloak, a cloak taken from the best sheepskins of a hundred families.

'With this cloak, no cold can harm you,' said the villagers.

Bawshou thanked them and walked on into the cold lands until he reached an icy river, broad as a sea.

'It is too much,' sighed Bawshou, and shook
his head. 'It cannot be crossed.'

'But your father crossed it,' said the golden phoenix.
'See the guiding star.'

The new star flickered from the other side.
Bawshou was afraid, but he stepped slowly
into the swirling water.

'Do not worry,' said the golden phoenix.
'The hundred-family cloak will keep you afloat.'

Bawshou fought the river.

He was hurled through the gorges of white water,
flung against rocks, swept along in a vast flood.

After many days he reached the other side,
but he was too weak to go on.

Villagers by the river gave him warmth, a bed
and something from their last food store
while he rested.

When he was strong enough to walk again
they gave him a special parcel of earth.

'You will need this,' they said.
'It comes from our hearts.'

Bawshou walked on until he came to an old
woman sitting at the junction of three roads.
'Granny, which way should I go to find the sun?'
Bawshou asked.

'Go home, young man,' the old woman said.
'The sun is dead.'

'No! I must go on. I must see the sun,
whether it is dead or alive.'

Soon he reached a strangely happy village, with people inviting him to join them in a banquet. They sang and laughed and offered him a cup of dark wine.

But the golden phoenix dropped into the cup a shoe made from a woman's flowing hair.

Bawshou leapt to his feet in rage. 'My father has died here!'

He hurled the poison cup at the ground and the village vanished as if it had never been.

Bawshou stopped and thought: the ghost village and the old woman were traps laid by the King of Devils. The home of the Devils must be close!

He strode across the great plain until he could hear the roar of the breakers of the East Ocean.

The new star was shimmering on the horizon, but the East Ocean was broader and deeper than all the rivers in the land. How could he cross this endless water?

Then Bawshou remembered the package of earth.

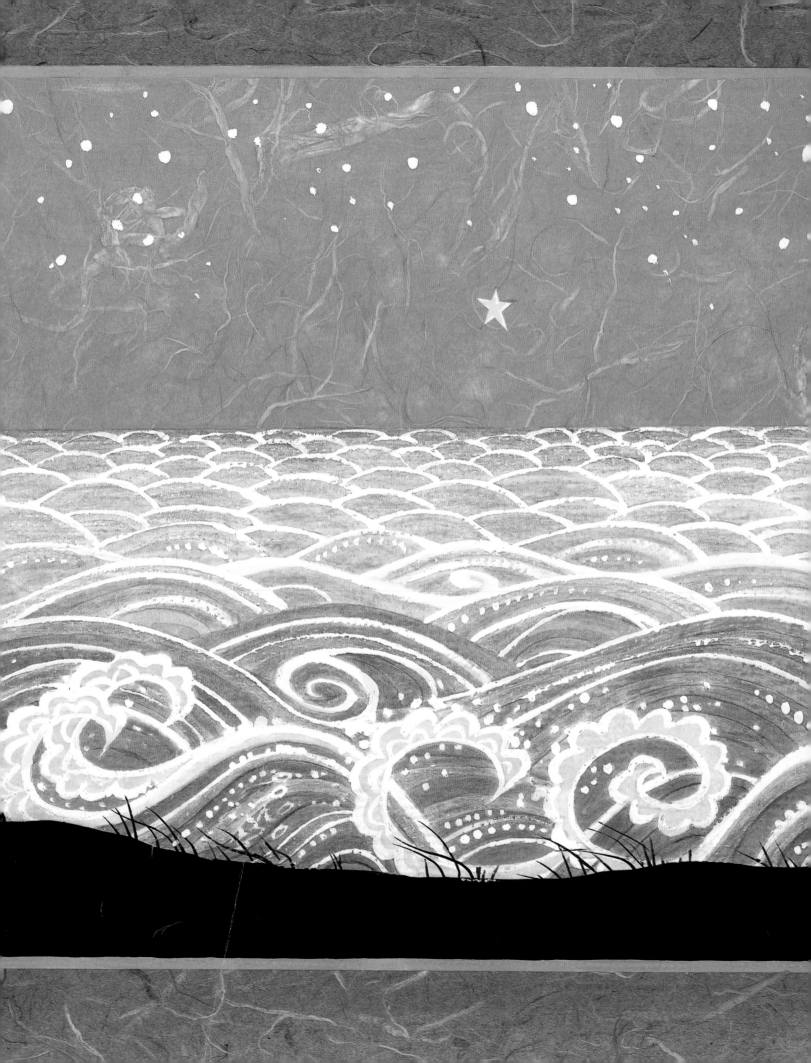

Bawshou threw a pinch of earth into the ocean and suddenly an island appeared.

A thousand pinches of earth became a thousand islands. Bawshou strode from island to island across the East Ocean.

He reached a black crag, alone in the ocean – the prison of the sun.

He crept up to the crag and heard the Devils laughing far below.

At last!

Bawshou filled his chest
with a great storm wind,
and roared into a cleft
in the crag.

The crag shook and
echoed Bawshou's anger,
as if the Earth was
cracking apart.

The Devils burst in panic
from their rock fortress,
tumbling into the sea.

Bawshou crept quietly
into the dark stone fortress.
He wandered down
dripping tunnels,
across still black lakes,
into caverns, silent
and waiting.

Then he saw a dim orange
light. A ball of dying
flame was flickering in
a cave deep under
the sea.

Bawshou had found the sun!

The golden phoenix supported the weight of the sun as Bawshou led them into the starlit night.

But the Devils swarmed after Bawshou and the sun, shrieking in rage.

The sun followed the bright new star, growing in size and power as it climbed from the sea.

The Devils howled and clutched at Bawshou, but the sun was driving back the black of the long night.

In the new morning the King of Devils was burnt from the sky.

And the sun brought light and warmth back to the Earth.

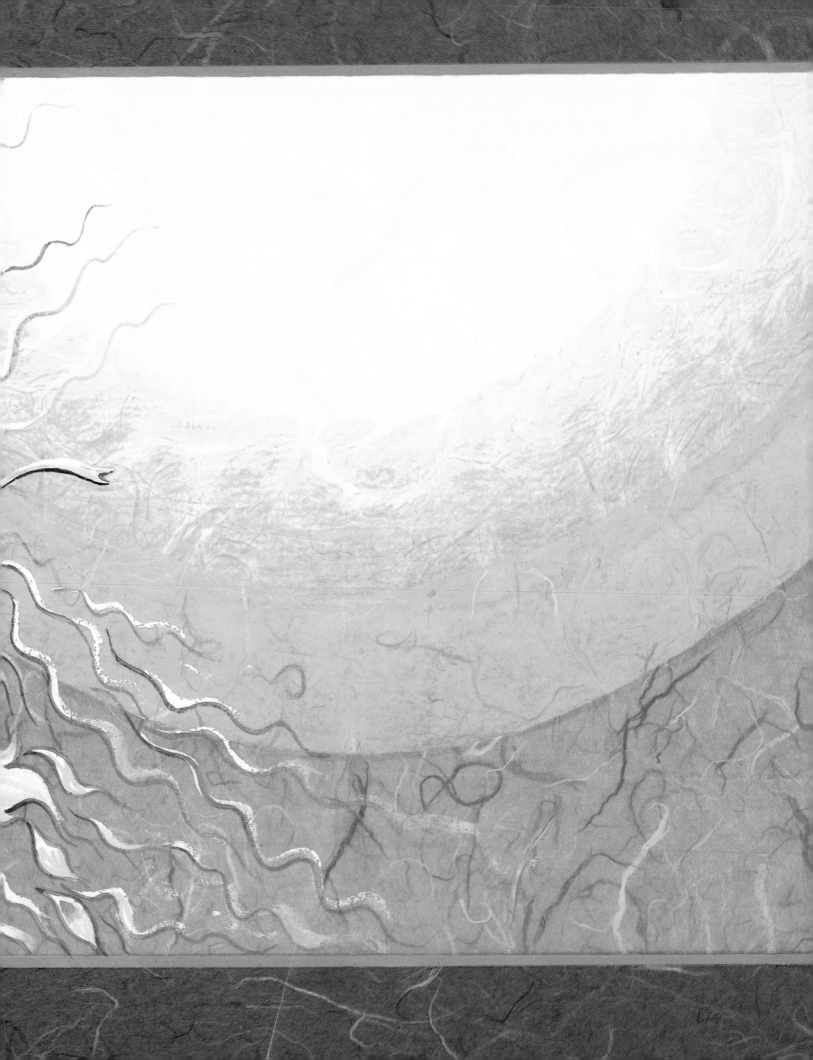

That is the way it was
thousands of years ago . . .

But when a pink-rimmed cloud
carries the sun into the sky at dawn,
that is the golden phoenix.

And there is a single bright star
that stays in the sky to greet the sun.
That is Bawshou's father, Liu Chun.

The West Lake in Eastern China
has a pagoda called Bawshou,
marking the place where Hui Niang
began her long wait for husband
and son.

That is the way it is.

For Joan Phipson,
who planted the seed – AB and CCY

For my mother,
with thanks for many years of encouragement – MP

Library of Congress Cataloging-in-Publication Data

Yeh, Chun-Chan.
    Bawshou rescues the sun/by Chun-Chan Yeh and Allan Baillie;
illustrated by Michelle Powell.
        p.   cm.
    Summary: When the King of the Devils steals the sun from the
sky, Bawshou goes on a magical journey to restore the light.
    ISBN 0-590-45453-6
    [1. Fairy tales. 2 Folklore—China.] I. Baillie, Allan.
    II. Powell, Michelle, ill. III. Title.
    PZ8.Y42Baw   1991
    398.21'0951—dc20   91-18960
                                                               CIP
                                                                AC

12 11 10 9 8 7 6 5 4 3 2 1   2 3 4 5 6 7/9

Printed in the U.S.A.   36

First Scholastic printing, April 1992